OFFICIAL

FEISTY Pets™

HANDBOOK

Everything you need to know!

WARNING:
FROM CUTE TO FEISTY
IN A SINGLE SQUEEZE!

Scholastic Inc.

Stock photos © Shutterstock: paper on page 3 (Sarah Kinnel); top of page 4 (Nik Merkulov); sticky note on page 5 (las100); push pin on page 5 and throughout (FabrikaSimf); star on page 5 and throughout (Sasha Ka); top of page 6 (Panuwach); photo corners on page 7 and throughout (LiliGraphie); paper and tape on page 7 and throughout (backUp); top of page 8 (K N); top of page 10 (Dotted Yeti); sticky note on page 11 and throughout (Picsfive); bottom of page 12 (Lio putra); heart on page 13 and throughout (Chinch); heart on page 15 and throughout (Cristian Barrios); headstone on page 15 and throughout (oscarporras); top of page 16 (Timmary); top of page 18 (Pikovit); top of page 20 (Roi and Roi); holly on page 21 and throughout (Mary Long); top of page 22 (Azuzl); top of page 24 (John T Takai); top of page 26 (Inked Pixels); top of page 28 (Sudowoodo); top of page 30 (Bhonard); bottom of page 30 (cobalt88); hat on page 32 (Wintakorn Choemnarong); top of page 34 (Superheang168); top of page 36 (Mara008); top of page 38 (Maria Averburg); ice cubes on page 39 (Talaj); top of page 40 (mixxxsh83); top of page 42 (Volodymyr Krasyuk); clouds on pages 42, 43 (AlexTanya); sign on page 49 (Mega Pixel); top of page 52 (Nerthuz); top of page 54 (sayu); top of page 56 (Dmitrii Kazitsyn); top of page 58 (NokHoOkNoi); top of page 60 (Andrey Lobachev); fish on page 63 and throughout (LAUDiseno); top of page 64 (gresei); sunglasses on page 66 (Vadelma); hamburgers on page 67 (stockcreations); top of page 68 (HN Works); top of page 72 (KAE CH); lights on pages 74, 75 (32 pixels); center of page 74 (LAUDiseno); top of page 78 (Oksancia); top of page 82 (Arno Jenkins); top of page 84 (Kristyna Vagnerova); top of page 86 (Chinch); top of page 88 (Shutterstock Vector); top of page 90 (HappyPictures).

ISBN 978-1-338-35860-5

10 9 8 7 6 5 4 3 2 1   19 20 21 22 23

Printed in the U.S.A.   40

First printing 2019

Book design by Mercedes Padró and Theresa Venezia

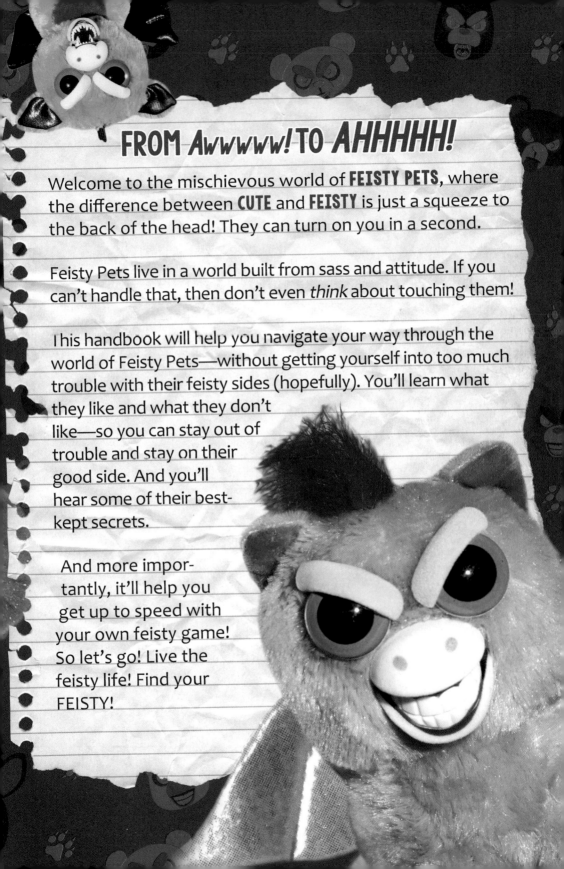

FROM *Awwwww!* TO *AHHHHH!*

Welcome to the mischievous world of **FEISTY PETS**, where the difference between **CUTE** and **FEISTY** is just a squeeze to the back of the head! They can turn on you in a second.

Feisty Pets live in a world built from sass and attitude. If you can't handle that, then don't even *think* about touching them!

This handbook will help you navigate your way through the world of Feisty Pets—without getting yourself into too much trouble with their feisty sides (hopefully). You'll learn what they like and what they don't like—so you can stay out of trouble and stay on their good side. And you'll hear some of their best-kept secrets.

And more importantly, it'll help you get up to speed with your own feisty game! So let's go! Live the feisty life! Find your FEISTY!

AKA: an alicorn

BIRTHDAY: February 29

LIKES: Manicures. Jalapeño peppers. Frenemies.

I WOULD ALWAYS . . . make sure my horn matches my hooves.

DISLIKES: Horses. Orange Jell-O. Daffodils.

I WOULD NEVER . . . fly coach.

FAVORITE FOOD: Anything that's as exotic as I am.

FAVORITE ACTIVITY: Ring toss.

WHAT EVERYBODY KNOWS: Alicorns have it all.

WHAT NOBODY KNOWS: It's hard to have it all.

BEST ADVICE: Always let your hoof polish dry before flying.

MOTTO/QUOTE: "Calling all unicorns! Calling all Pegasi! It's time to come together and STOP THE MADNESS!"

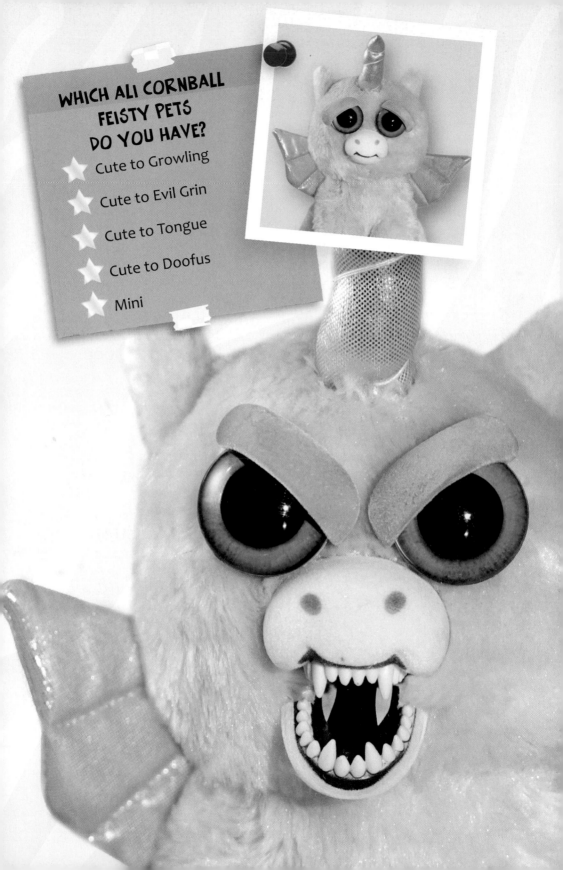

WHICH ALI CORNBALL
FEISTY PETS
DO YOU HAVE?

⭐ Cute to Growling

⭐ Cute to Evil Grin

⭐ Cute to Tongue

⭐ Cute to Doofus

⭐ Mini

NAME: Billy Blubberbutt

AKA: a narwhal

BIRTHDAY: April 22

LIKES: Fencing. Spearfishing. Cuddling.

I WOULD ALWAYS . . . use my horn for good . . . unlike those evil unicorns.

DISLIKES: Unicorns. Soccer. Root canals.

I WOULD NEVER . . . hang out with Glenda Glitterpoop!

FAVORITE FOOD: *Ship* kebabs.

FAVORITE ACTIVITY: Sword fighting.

WHAT EVERYBODY ~~KNOWS:~~ Should Know I don't have a horn. I have a tusk, which is actually a tooth! I'm not some kind of unicorn fantasy.

WHAT NOBODY KNOWS: I actually exist, unlike those wannabe unicorns.

BEST ADVICE: Never trust a unicorn.

MOTTO/QUOTE: "I'm the Jedi of the sea."

WHICH BILLY BLUBBERBUTT FEISTY PETS DO YOU HAVE?

🐾 Cute to Growling

🐾 Cute to Evil Grin

🐾 Cute to Tongue

🐾 Cute to Doofus

🐾 Mini

NAME: Black Belt Bobby

AKA: a panda

BIRTHDAY: March 16

LIKES: Black eyes. Martial arts movies. Chocolate-covered bamboo.

I WOULD ALWAYS . . . recommend heavy eyeliner.

DISLIKES: Other pandas. Rainbows. Exercise.

I WOULD NEVER . . . want to be a polar bear!

FAVORITE FOOD: Oreos.

FAVORITE ACTIVITY: Riding on ceiling fans.

WHAT EVERYBODY KNOWS: I'm the man of the house!

WHAT NOBODY KNOWS: I actually do whatever my wife says or wants.

BEST ADVICE: Feisty is as feisty does. Now get lost!

MOTTO/QUOTE: "Do you wanna get fluffed up? Well, do ya? Punk!"

WHICH BLACK BELT BOBBY FEISTY PETS DO YOU HAVE?

 Cute to Growling

 Cute to Evil Grin

 Cute to Tongue

 Cute to Doofus

 Mini

NAME: Brainless Brian

AKA: a triceratops

BIRTHDAY: 65 million years ago

LIKES: Classic prehistoric music. Long stomps on the beach. Hide-and-seek.

I WOULD ALWAYS . . . go retro.

DISLIKES: Paleontologists. Asteroids. Modern times.

I WOULD NEVER . . . invite a tyrannosaurus to lunch.

FAVORITE FOOD: Jurassic pork.

FAVORITE ACTIVITY: Terrifying small children and then pulling out a salad for lunch.

WHAT EVERYBODY KNOWS: Three horns are better than two.

WHAT NOBODY KNOWS: I have never met Steven Spielberg.

BEST ADVICE: You're only as extinct as you think you are.

MOTTO/QUOTE: "Don't be a TRYceratops, be a DOceratops!"

AKA: a basset hound

BIRTHDAY: May 17

LIKES: Pessimists. Movie marathons. Eating poo.

I WOULD ALWAYS . . . trust my nose.

DISLIKES: Optimists. Superheroes. Not eating poo.

I WOULD NEVER . . . say no to a snack, especially a smelly one.

FAVORITE FOOD: Whatever smells the most at any given moment.

FAVORITE ACTIVITY: Endless hours wandering museums.

WHAT EVERYBODY KNOWS: I will only listen to you if you have a treat.

WHAT NOBODY KNOWS: Gravity gets me a little down.

BEST ADVICE: Don't ever call me a beagle!

MOTTO/QUOTE: "Dear God, thank you for the food I'm about to steal."

WHICH BUFORD BUTTSNIFFER FEISTY PETS DO YOU HAVE?

♥ Cute to Growling

♥ Cute to Evil Grin

♥ Cute to Tongue

♥ Cute to Doofus

♥ Mini

13

NAME: Cuddles Von Rumblestrut

AKA: a guinea pig

BIRTHDAY: July 16

LIKES: Eating homework. Heavy metal. Cliff diving.

I WOULD ALWAYS . . . hang out with Lightning Bolt Lenny, a slow-moving, cliff-diving sloth . . . what could be better?

DISLIKES: Hamster wheels. Sharing. Science experiments.

I WOULD NEVER . . . have thought I would be run over by a monster truck!

FAVORITE FOOD: Anything smaller than me.

FAVORITE ACTIVITY: Chewin' the stuffing out of silly plushes.

WHAT EVERYBODY ~~KNOWS~~: *Should Know* Guinea pigs know how to strut.

WHAT NOBODY KNOWS: Guinea pigs would rule the world if they were just a teeny bit bigger.

BEST ADVICE: Ladies love the strut.

MOTTO/QUOTE: "I came, I saw, I pooped everywhere!"

DO YOU HAVE A CUDDLES
VON RUMBLESTRUT
FEISTY PET?

Cute to Growling

R.I.P.
The Third
to Fall.

NAME: Dastardly Daniel

AKA: a horned owl

BIRTHDAY: September 26

LIKES: Pizza delivery. Rodents for dinner. Anarchy.

I WOULD ALWAYS . . . order pepperoni, olives, and rats (but I would never tip the delivery guy).

DISLIKES: Speed limit signs. Bedtime. Ceiling fans.

I WOULD NEVER . . . want to be a wizard's pet.

FAVORITE FOOD: Whatever I can steal from the snowy owls.

FAVORITE ACTIVITY: Watching snowy owls trying to blend in in the forest.

WHAT EVERYBODY KNOWS: Snowy owls aren't even wise . . .

WHAT NOBODY KNOWS: I'm afraid of the dark.

BEST ADVICE to snowy owls: Make sure you wear a bib. (Babies!)

MOTTO/QUOTE: "Snowy owls ask too many questions."

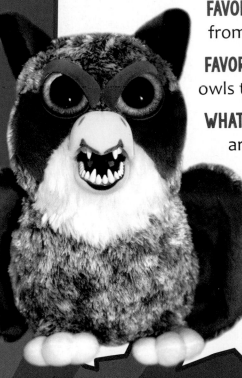

NAME: Dolly Llama

AKA: a llama

BIRTHDAY: July 6

LIKES: Temporary tattoos. Spitting. Wool sweaters.

I WOULD ALWAYS . . . be kind to those who worship me.

DISLIKES: Alpacas. Meditation. Silence.

I WOULD NEVER . . . spit unless provoked. Then I would definitely spit. (And feel good about it.)

FAVORITE FOOD: Zucchini, carrots, pizza, egg rolls (or anything else with a double letter, obviously!)

FAVORITE ACTIVITY: Wearing alpaca sweaters in front of alpacas.

WHAT EVERYBODY KNOWS: Camels are very proud to be related to llamas. Llamas agree that camels should feel proud.

WHAT NOBODY KNOWS: My code name is Barack *Ollama*.

BEST ADVICE: Oooooooooohhhhmmmmm. *Not!*

MOTTO/QUOTE: "Save your llama from the drama."

WHICH DOLLY LLAMA FEISTY PETS DO YOU HAVE?

- 🐾 Cute to Growling
- 🐾 Cute to Evil Grin
- 🐾 Cute to Tongue
- 🐾 Cute to Doofus
- 🐾 Mini

NAME: Ebeneezer Claws

AKA: a Santa bear

BIRTHDAY: December 25

LIKES: Taking candy from babies. Lumps of coal. Halloween.

I WOULD ALWAYS . . . use the chimney to break into your house.

DISLIKES: Elves. Mistletoe. The giving spirit.

I WOULD NEVER . . . lose a night's sleep just to fly around the world delivering presents. Bah!

FAVORITE FOOD: Candy that used to belong to babies.

FAVORITE ACTIVITY: Impersonating Santa.

WHAT EVERYBODY KNOWS: I hate the North Pole.

WHAT NOBODY KNOWS: I was on the "Nice" list once.

BEST ADVICE: Get used to the coal and have a good time!

MOTTO/QUOTE: "Hey, Santa! I'm naughty AND nice!"

NAUGHTY / NICE

WHICH EBENEEZER CLAWS
FEISTY PETS DO YOU HAVE?

- Cute to Growling
- Cute to Evil Grin
- Cute to Tongue
- Cute to Doofus
- Mini

21

NAME: Evil Eden

AKA: a horse

BIRTHDAY: November 21

LIKES: Unlatched gates. Westerns. Your vegetable garden.

I WOULD ALWAYS . . . latch your gate for you after I've eaten your garden down to just dirty nubs.

DISLIKES: Saddles. Cowboys. Unicorns.

I WOULD NEVER . . . put a saddle on you and take you for a spin.

FAVORITE FOOD: Anything with *ranch* dressing.

FAVORITE ACTIVITY: Staying up late, because I'm a night*mare.*

WHAT EVERYBODY KNOWS: *Evil* spelled backward is *live.* (Sure, it doesn't matter. But it's still true and everybody knows it.)

WHAT NOBODY KNOWS: I asked for a little girl for Christmas.

BEST ADVICE: I'd like to say something, but I'm a little *horse.*

MOTTO/QUOTE: "Unicorns lie."

WHICH EVIL EDEN FEISTY
PETS DO YOU HAVE?

🐾 Cute to Growling

🐾 Cute to Evil Grin

🐾 Cute to Tongue

🐾 Cute to Doofus

🐾 Mini

23

NAME: Extinct Eddie

AKA: a stegosaurus

BIRTHDAY: 163 million years ago

LIKES: Breakfast time. Lunchtime. Dinnertime.

I WOULD ALWAYS . . . clean my plates.

DISLIKES: Museums. Fossils. Mammals.

I WOULD NEVER . . . tease the elderly.

FAVORITE FOOD: Dino-*s'mores*.

FAVORITE ACTIVITY: Not being eaten by a T. rex.

WHAT EVERYBODY KNOWS: Fossils rock!

WHAT NOBODY KNOWS: I sell meteor insurance.

BEST ADVICE: Playing leap-frog with a stegosaurus is a bad idea.

MOTTO/QUOTE: "Scientists have determined that death was the number one killer of dinosaurs!"

WHICH EXTINCT EDDIE FEISTY PETS DO YOU HAVE?

🐾 Cute to Growling

🐾 Cute to Evil Grin

🐾 Cute to Tongue

🐾 Cute to Doofus

🐾 Mini

NAME: Ferdinand Flamefart

AKA: a dragon

BIRTHDAY: January 16

LIKES: Burning stuff. Damsels in distress. Roasting marshmallows.

I WOULD ALWAYS . . . pop bubble wrap.

DISLIKES: Firefighters. Airplanes. Knights.

I WOULD NEVER . . . play with fire extinguishers . . . it's dangerous!

FAVORITE FOOD: Medieval knights.

FAVORITE ACTIVITY: Foiling Super Doofus's plans.

WHAT EVERYBODY KNOWS: I love all my meat flame broiled.

WHAT NOBODY KNOWS: I have postnasal drip.

BEST ADVICE: Never ask a dragon to blow out the candles on a birthday cake.

MOTTO/QUOTE:
"Curse you, Super Doofus!"

WHICH FERDINAND FLAMEFART FEISTY PETS DO YOU HAVE?

- Cute to Growling
- Cute to Evil Grin
- Cute to Tongue
- Cute to Doofus
- Mini

27

NAME: Freddy Wreckingball

AKA: a dog

BIRTHDAY: July 9

LIKES: Trash talking. Bones. Cats (they taste like chicken).

I WOULD ALWAYS . . . eat anything that tastes like chicken.

DISLIKES: Veterinarians. Cyclists. Hugs.

I WOULD NEVER . . . watch cat videos online.

FAVORITE FOOD: Anything blue.

FAVORITE ACTIVITY: Riding that big wrecking ball in the sky.

WHAT EVERYBODY KNOWS: Dogs do more with one life than cats do with nine! DOGS RULE!

WHAT NOBODY KNOWS: Sammy Suckerpunch wants to be me— POSER!

BEST ADVICE: Avoid wrecking balls ridden by pop stars.

MOTTO/QUOTE: "I love you . . . but it's a TOUGH love!"

R.I.P.
The First
to Fall.

DO YOU HAVE A
FREDDY WRECKINGBALL
FEISTY PET?

💔 Cute to Growling

NAME: Ginormous Gracie

AKA: a giraffe

BIRTHDAY: June 21

LIKES: Webcams. Sunroofs. Leg warmers.

I WOULD ALWAYS . . . run with scissors!

DISLIKES: Whiplash. Infinity scarves. Meerkats.

I WOULD NEVER . . . wear a turtleneck.

FAVORITE FOOD: Anything tall, green, and leafy.

FAVORITE ACTIVITY: Takin' selfies while doing 80 mph in a convertible!

WHAT EVERYBODY KNOWS: I am ginormously photogenic.

WHAT NOBODY KNOWS: I've never played basketball. Giraffe dudes call me "shorty."

BEST ADVICE: Constant social media is not good for you. So smash your screen and you won't see anything!

MOTTO/QUOTE: "Don't be a pain in the neck!"

WHICH GINORMOUS GRACIE FEISTY PETS DO YOU HAVE?

🐾 Cute to Growling

🐾 Cute to Evil Grin

🐾 Cute to Tongue

🐾 Cute to Doofus

🐾 Mini

AKA: a unicorn

BIRTHDAY: October 11

LIKES: Slime. Myself. Rapping.

I WOULD ALWAYS . . . do your makeup—for any occasion!

DISLIKES: Little children. World peace. Lollipops.

I WOULD NEVER . . . leave the house without my Feisty Fierce brand of makeup on.

FAVORITE FOOD: Whatever matches my outfit the best.

FAVORITE ACTIVITY: Fashion consulting and vlogging.

WHAT EVERYBODY KNOWS: Pink is totes last season.

WHAT NOBODY KNOWS: I taught Beyoncé how to dance and sing.

BEST ADVICE: You can never have too much contouring. Use Feisty Fierce makeup to make your dreams come true!

MOTTO/QUOTE: "I feel like nobody believes in me. Little white pony is OUT! BYYYYYE!"

WHICH GLENDA GLITTERPOOP FEISTY PETS DO YOU HAVE?

♥ Cute to Growling

♥ Cute to Evil Grin

♥ Cute to Tongue

♥ Cute to Doofus

♥ Mini

AKA: a monkey

BIRTHDAY: April 7

LIKES: Jungle gyms. Bananas. Throwing poo.

I WOULD ALWAYS . . . throw poo.

DISLIKES: Stuffed animals. Global warming. Your face!

I WOULD NEVER . . . sniff butts. (Although I do enjoy throwing poo.)

FAVORITE FOOD: I'm a cop, so what do you think?! Donuts, of course!

FAVORITE ACTIVITY: Putting pesky jaywalkers behind bars.

WHAT EVERYBODY KNOWS: I am the real Brad Pitt.

WHAT NOBODY KNOWS: I'm not a real cop—I just play one on YouTube.

BEST ADVICE: You darn kids . . . stop breaking the law!

MOTTO/QUOTE: "Livin' the feisty life!"

WHICH GRANDMASTER FUNK
FEISTY PETS DO YOU HAVE?

🐾 Cute to Growling

🐾 Cute to Evil Grin

🐾 Cute to Tongue

🐾 Cute to Doofus

🐾 Mini

AKA: a snowy owl

BIRTHDAY: June 28

LIKES: Lunar eclipses. Creepy old castles. Magic shows.

I WOULD ALWAYS . . . keep the light on.

DISLIKES: The dark. Walruses. Fantasy stories.

I WOULD NEVER . . . wanna be horned.

FAVORITE FOOD: Anything I catch.

FAVORITE ACTIVITY: Watching horned owls try to catch food in the snow.

WHAT EVERYBODY KNOWS: I don't give a hoot about horned owls!

WHAT NOBODY KNOWS: I don't deliver mail.

BEST ADVICE to horned owls: Get a grip. They are tufts, not horns.

MOTTO/QUOTE: "Hoo-Hoo. What-What. Where-Where. When-When. Why-Why."

WHICH HENRY WHODUNNIT FEISTY PETS DO YOU HAVE?

🐾 Cute to Growling

🐾 Cute to Evil Grin

🐾 Cute to Tongue

🐾 Cute to Doofus

🐾 Mini

NAME: Ice Cold Izzy

AKA: a penguin

BIRTHDAY: April 25

LIKES: Waddling. Big-wave surfing. Tuxedos.

I WOULD ALWAYS . . . go an extra mile for an egg.

DISLIKES: Big seals with pointy teeth. Sunburns. Scrambled eggs.

I WOULD NEVER . . . worry about my waistline. (Get serious. I can't even find it.)

FAVORITE FOOD: Ice*bergers* and *brrrr*itos.

FAVORITE ACTIVITY: Going to a *dive*-in theatre.

WHAT EVERYBODY KNOWS: It's good to be the middle guy when it's 125 degrees below zero. Huddle up, yo!

WHAT NOBODY KNOWS: I ♥ dance.

BEST ADVICE: Money can't buy happiness, but it can buy a penguin. Have you ever seen a sad person with a penguin?

MOTTO/QUOTE: "Not everything black and white is wearing a tuxedo!"

AKA: a kangaroo

BIRTHDAY: May 15

LIKES: Kickboxing. Pocket protectors. Tropical fish.

I WOULD ALWAYS . . . kick my kid out of the pouch to make room for my cell phone.

DISLIKES: The British monarchy. Papier-mâché. Liza Loca.

I WOULD NEVER . . . set foot in New Zealand.

FAVORITE FOOD: Jumping beans.

FAVORITE ACTIVITY: Hangin' out in bouncy houses.

WHAT EVERYBODY KNOWS: Bunnies wish they were kangaroos.

WHAT NOBODY KNOWS: I hate posers on trampolines acting like they can jump.

BEST ADVICE: Always name your children "Joey."

MOTTO/QUOTE: "Some mother you are!"

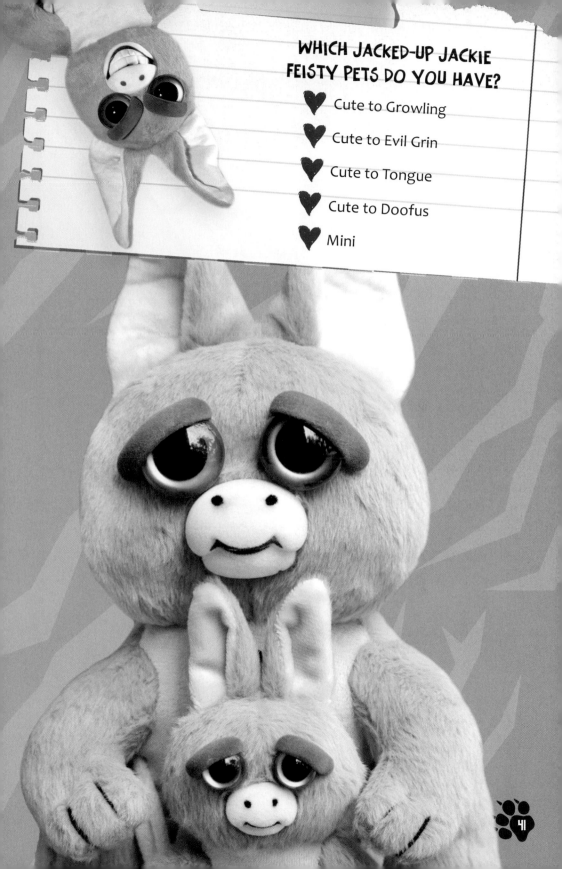

WHICH JACKED-UP JACKIE FEISTY PETS DO YOU HAVE?

♥ Cute to Growling

♥ Cute to Evil Grin

♥ Cute to Tongue

♥ Cute to Doofus

♥ Mini

AKA: A GOAT!

BIRTHDAY: JUNE 10

LIKES: YOUR LAWN! ARM WRESTLING! KNOCK-KNOCK JOKES!

I WOULD ALWAYS . . . GIVE UNWANTED ADVICE!

DISLIKES: PETTING ZOOS! BARBED WIRE! GOAT CHEESE!

I WOULD NEVER . . . SPEAK QUIETLY!

FAVORITE FOOD: WHEN I WAS YOUR AGE, WE DIDN'T HAVE FOOD!

FAVORITE ACTIVITY: REMINDING PEOPLE HOW WIMPY THEY ARE COMPARED TO ME!

WHAT EVERYBODY KNOWS: I DISLIKE CHILDREN!

WHAT NOBODY KNOWS: I ATE THE ORIGINAL DRAFT OF THE UNITED STATES CONSTITUTION!

"JUST DO IT! MAKE YOUR DREAMS COME TRUE!"

AKA: a polar bear

BIRTHDAY: February 27

LIKES: Ice fishing. Taking selfies. Yellow snow.

I WOULD ALWAYS . . . post selfies on Instagram.

DISLIKES: Springtime. Fuzzy white seals. Lawyers.

I WOULD NEVER . . . photobomb a selfie.

FAVORITE FOOD: Igloos—when they have people inside!

FAVORITE ACTIVITY: Looking in the mirror.

WHAT EVERYBODY KNOWS: I'm the supreme predator of the Arctic, baby!

WHAT NOBODY KNOWS: I once ate a Christmas elf.

BEST ADVICE: Before approaching a predator, ask yourself, "Do I feel lucky?"

MOTTO/QUOTE: "If it's white and fluffy, I want it."

44

WHICH KARL THE SNARL FEISTY PETS DO YOU HAVE?

- Cute to Growling
- Cute to Evil Grin
- Cute to Tongue
- Cute to Doofus
- Mini

FEISTY FASHION!

TIARAS AND TRESSES

PAJAMA CHIC!

SLOTH IN A BASEBALL CAP!

BEAUTY AND THE BEAST

BOWS & BAUBLES

SUPERHERO STYLIN'!

GANGSTA!

HATTY BIRTHDAY STYLE!

FAIRY-TALE FEISTY

CLOWNWEAR

MERMAID MODELING

GOTH FEISTY

FEISTY FRIENDS!

BESTIES!

FERDINAND FLAMEFART + SPARKLES RAINBOWBARF

MAGICAL CREATURES!

DA BEARS!

CAT-O-CLYSMIC!

HORNS A PLENTY

This is a tusk, not a horn!

49

FEISTY FUNNIES!

I LOVE TOURISTS!

Q: What sign did Karl the Snarl post when he got hungry for lunch?

A: "TOURISTS WELCOME"

Q: What is Princess Pottymouth's dream car?

A: A *Fur*rari.

Q: What did Jacked-Up Jackie call her Joey when he wouldn't get out and hop by himself?

A: A *pouch* potato!

Q: What did Junkyard Jeff say when the other Feisties said they didn't want to hear any more knock-knock jokes?

A: "You have *goat* to be kidding me!"

THAT'S NOT PUNNY.

Q: Why can't Lethal Lena ever play hide-and-seek?

A: Because she's always spotted!

I CAN SEE THAT.

Q: What do you call Ginormous Gracie when she goes to the lake and floats in the water?

A: A Gir*raft*.

Q: What do you call Grandmaster Funk when he puts on a wizard's outfit?

A: *Hairy* Potter.

Q: What would you get if you gave Lightning Bolt Lenny a sharp stick?

A: A slow*poke*.

SLOTH HUMOR . . . YOU MIGHT NOT GET IT RIGHT AWAY.

AKA: a black cat

BIRTHDAY: October 31

LIKES: Ding-dong ditching. Dumpster diving. Black licorice.

I WOULD ALWAYS . . . choose trouble.

DISLIKES: Daylight. Superheroes. Pumpkins.

I WOULD NEVER . . . consider orange the new black.

FAVORITE FOOD: Candy stolen from trick-or-treaters.

FAVORITE ACTIVITY: Crossing my frenemies' paths.

WHAT EVERYBODY KNOWS: Tricks are more fun than treats.

WHAT NOBODY KNOWS: I worship Darth Vader.

BEST ADVICE: Never take the high road.

MOTTO/QUOTE: "Black cats against bad luck!"

WHICH KATY COBWEB FEISTY PETS DO YOU HAVE?

🐾 Cute to Growling

🐾 Cute to Evil Grin

🐾 Cute to Tongue

🐾 Cute to Doofus

🐾 Mini

53

NAME: Lady Monstertruck

AKA: a pink cat

BIRTHDAY: September 8

LIKES: Selfies. Paparazzi. Black nail polish.

I WOULD ALWAYS . . . tease and annoy a dog.

DISLIKES: Laser pointers. Sofa cushions. Curtains.

I WOULD NEVER . . . destroy the curtains unless I've already ripped apart every pillow in the room.

FAVORITE FOOD: I love chasing and killing laser pointers.

FAVORITE ACTIVITY: Traveling the highways and byways.

WHAT EVERYBODY KNOWS: You can always find me in a crowd.

WHAT NOBODY KNOWS: Pink is NOT my favorite color.

BEST ADVICE: Don't get run over by a monster truck.

MOTTO/QUOTE: "I came, I saw, I complained."

NAME: Lethal Lena

AKA: a snow leopard

BIRTHDAY: October 23

LIKES: Unwary hikers. Olympic bobsledding. Cat toys.

I WOULD ALWAYS . . . steal toys from innocent kittens.

DISLIKES: Snowmen. Men. All other animals.

I WOULD NEVER . . . play catch with a narwhal. (Horns are bad news for balls.)

FAVORITE FOOD: The egos of men.

FAVORITE ACTIVITY: Man-hating.

WHAT EVERYBODY KNOWS: I don't like coffee.

WHAT NOBODY KNOWS: I'm cold on the outside but on the inside . . . Oh, who am I kidding? I'm cold on the inside too!

BEST ADVICE: Never trust a man.

MOTTO/QUOTE: "I like my coffee like I like my men— far, far away from me."

WHICH LETHAL LENA FEISTY PETS DO YOU HAVE?

🐾 Cute to Growling

🐾 Cute to Evil Grin

🐾 Cute to Tongue

🐾 Cute to Doofus

🐾 Mini

AKA: a sloth

BIRTHDAY: October 20

LIKES: Cliff diving. Naptime. Drag racing.

I WOULD ALWAYS . . . hang around.

DISLIKES: Coffee. Aerobics. Romantic comedies.

I WOULD NEVER . . . let anyone call me a TWO-toed sloth!

FAVORITE FOOD: A steady diet of nonsense and shenanigans.

FAVORITE ACTIVITY: Reporting all the feisty facts, and only the feisty facts.

WHAT EVERYBODY KNOWS: I would never be seen on TV without a sporty tie.

WHAT NOBODY KNOWS: I secretly love glitter.

BEST ADVICE: Don't judge a sloth by its toe count.

MOTTO/QUOTE: "I think . . . I might be . . . getting . . . angry . . . . nope . . . too much . . . trouble. Back to sleep."

WHICH LIGHTNING BOLT LENNY FEISTY PETS DO YOU HAVE?

- 🐾 Cute to Growling
- 🐾 Cute to Evil Grin
- 🐾 Cute to Tongue
- 🐾 Cute to Doofus
- 🐾 Mini

NAME: Liza Loca

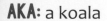

AKA: a koala

BIRTHDAY: March 31

LIKES: Dollar stores. Guys named "David." Feisty Films.

I WOULD ALWAYS . . . love Liza Koshy.

DISLIKES: Fake eyebrows. Distracted drivers. Anything that costs more than $1.

I WOULD NEVER . . . pay more than a dollar for anything.

FAVORITE FOOD: COFFEE!!!!

FAVORITE ACTIVITY: Shopping at the dollar store.

WHAT EVERYBODY KNOWS: "Little" and "cute" can be misleading.

WHAT NOBODY KNOWS: I'm just a little koala with big dreams.

BEST ADVICE: Never trust a boy with your heart.

MOTTO/QUOTE: "Little brown koala is out!"

WHICH LIZA LOCA FEISTY PETS DO YOU HAVE?

- ♥ Cute to Growling
- ♥ Cute to Evil Grin
- ♥ Cute to Tongue
- ♥ Cute to Doofus
- ♥ Mini

NAME: Louie Ladykiller

AKA: a turtle

BIRTHDAY: May 23

LIKES: Racecars. Snowboarding. Video Games.

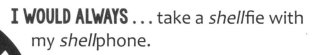

I WOULD ALWAYS . . . take a *shell*fie with my *shell*phone.

DISLIKES: Hares. Shell shock. Sloths.

I WOULD NEVER . . . go anywhere with Lightning Bolt Lenny.

FAVORITE FOOD: Peanut butter and jelly*fish*.

FAVORITE ACTIVITY: Turning upside down on my shell and pretending I'm flying.

WHAT EVERYBODY KNOWS: I'm not really a ninja.

WHAT NOBODY KNOWS: What goes on inside my shell. (And I would prefer to keep it that way.)

BEST ADVICE: Always be slow to anger.

MOTTO/QUOTE: "Speed is my middle name. I just never use it because it takes too long."

WHICH LOUIE LADYKILLER FEISTY PETS DO YOU HAVE?

- Cute to Growling
- Cute to Evil Grin
- Cute to Tongue
- Cute to Doofus
- Mini

63

NAME: Lunatic Lexi

AKA: a golden doodle

BIRTHDAY: April 1

LIKES: Gluten. Science fiction. Makeup tutorials.

I WOULD ALWAYS . . . chase first, ask second.

DISLIKES: Blonde jokes. Ballroom dancing. Perms.

I WOULD NEVER . . . play fetch—it's a pointless game.

FAVORITE FOOD: People's shoes.

FAVORITE ACTIVITY: Making cats curious (since it kills them).

WHAT EVERYBODY KNOWS: My computer has a lot of bites on it.

WHAT NOBODY KNOWS: I was the runner-up to play Chewbacca.

BEST ADVICE: If you can't eat it or play with it, just pee on it and walk away.

MOTTO/QUOTE: "I don't always bark at night, but when I do, it's for no reason."

WHICH LUNATIC LEXI
FEISTY PETS DO YOU HAVE?

🐾 Cute to Growling

🐾 Cute to Evil Grin

🐾 Cute to Tongue

🐾 Cute to Doofus

🐾 Mini

AKA: a lion

BIRTHDAY: June 16

LIKES: Pro wrestling. Meerkats (they taste like chicken). Steak wrapped in bacon.

I WOULD ALWAYS . . . have dinner with Ginormous Gracie, since she hates meerkats . . . more for me!

DISLIKES: House cats. Hairbrushes. Siri.

I WOULD NEVER . . . sleep without an eye mask and hair net.

FAVORITE FOOD: Nerdburgers with a side order of zebra.

FAVORITE ACTIVITY: Going out with my imaginary girlfriend.

WHAT EVERYBODY KNOWS: Siri has it in for me.

WHAT NOBODY KNOWS: Siri actually has a crush on me.

BEST ADVICE: Never trust a "smart" phone.

MOTTO/QUOTE: "Feisty is what they call me when I'm in a GOOD mood!"

WHICH MARKY MISCHIEF FEISTY PETS DO YOU HAVE?

- Cute to Growling
- Cute to Evil Grin
- Cute to Tongue
- Cute to Doofus
- Mini

AKA: a calico cat

BIRTHDAY: September 9

LIKES: Black jelly beans. Banjo music. Talent shows.

I WOULD ALWAYS . . . scratch out a living.

DISLIKES: Sweating. Stop signs. Low riders.

I WOULD NEVER . . . run a marathon if I couldn't find a shortcut.

FAVORITE FOOD: *Mice* Krispies.

FAVORITE ACTIVITY: Unrolling toilet paper rolls.

WHAT EVERYBODY KNOWS: I'm the most talented cat you've ever met.

WHAT NOBODY KNOWS: I'm really a dog person.

BEST ADVICE: Always look both ways before crossing the highway.

MOTTO/QUOTE: "Don't be a copycat!"

WHICH MARY MONSTERTRUCK FEISTY PETS DO YOU HAVE?

♥ Cute to Growling

♥ Cute to Evil Grin

♥ Cute to Tongue

♥ Cute to Doofus

♥ Mini

California FEISTY

AKA: a tabby cat

BIRTHDAY: November 4

LIKES: Sugar and preservatives. Pranking. Sleeping in.

I WOULD ALWAYS . . . eat sugar and preservatives!

DISLIKES: Butterflies. Valentine's Day. People.

I WOULD NEVER . . . eat anything organic.

FAVORITE FOOD: Butterflies.

FAVORITE ACTIVITY: Driving in my convertible and feeling the wind in my pottymouth.

WHAT EVERYBODY KNOWS: My name might be "Princess," but I consider myself QUEEN of the Feisty Pets!

WHAT NOBODY KNOWS: How many lives I have left. I don't even know—maybe I'm on my ninth, or maybe I'm on my third. So, you gotta ask yourself, is it worth annoying the princess and getting on her bad side for half a dozen more lives? (That's a lotta lives!)

BEST ADVICE: Eat chemical preservatives and artificial sweeteners ONLY!

MOTTO/QUOTE: "Life is a box of chocolates—eat them all!"

WHICH PRINCESS POTTYMOUTH FEISTY PETS DO YOU HAVE?

⭐ Cute to Growling

⭐ Cute to Evil Grin

⭐ Cute to Tongue

⭐ Cute to Doofus

⭐ Mini

NAME: Rascal Rampage

AKA: a raccoon

BIRTHDAY: October 1

LIKES: Junk food. Burgling. Trash.

I WOULD ALWAYS . . . wash my hands before eating.

DISLIKES: The garbage disposal. The truth. Your dog.

I WOULD NEVER . . . go anywhere without my mask.

FAVORITE FOOD: Whatever the trash can is serving. It's my favorite restaurant.

FAVORITE ACTIVITY: Making ransom demand videos.

WHAT EVERYBODY KNOWS: Masked bandits have more fun.

WHAT NOBODY KNOWS: I actually wash my hands before I eat my trash.

BEST ADVICE: Stay feisty, my friends!

MOTTO/QUOTE: "Yo. You wanna bounce?"

WHICH RASCAL RAMPAGE FEISTY PETS DO YOU HAVE?

 Cute to Growling

 Cute to Evil Grin

 Cute to Tongue

 Cute to Doofus

 Mini

NAME: Rude Alf

AKA: a reindeer

BIRTHDAY: July 27

LIKES: Breaking and entering. Drones. Skydiving.

I WOULD ALWAYS . . . use my nose for good . . . unless I didn't feel like it.

DISLIKES: Grandma. Facial hair. Slippery roofs.

I WOULD NEVER . . . join in any reindeer games!

FAVORITE FOOD: Santa's cookies.

FAVORITE ACTIVITY: Watching other reindeer try to find their way in the dark.

WHAT EVERYBODY KNOWS: Santa would be nobody without me.

WHAT NOBODY KNOWS: Santa replaced me with a GPS sleigh-guiding app. (So, I'm a little angry!)

BEST ADVICE: Never laugh and call me names!

MOTTO/QUOTE: "I sleigh every day, bro!"

WHICH RUDE ALF FEISTY PETS DO YOU HAVE?

- Cute to Growling
- Cute to Evil Grin
- Cute to Tongue
- Cute to Doofus
- Mini

NAME: Sammy Suckerpunch

AKA: a Siberian husky

BIRTHDAY: August 26

LIKES: Sniffing butts. Eating crayons. Napping in the laundry.

I WOULD ALWAYS . . . sniff your butt.

DISLIKES: Bath time. My tail. Your mama!

I WOULD NEVER . . . say no to poo.

FAVORITE FOODS: I love poo and vomit.

FAVORITE ACTIVITY: Hanging out in the scratch-n-sniff aisle at the card shop.

WHAT EVERYBODY KNOWS: I like sniffing butts.

WHAT NOBODY KNOWS: I love vacuum cleaners.

WISE WORDS: Sniff butts every day!

MOTTO/QUOTE: "I'm not begging anymore. Give me the food!"

WHICH SAMMY SUCKERPUNCH FEISTY PETS DO YOU HAVE?

♥ Cute to Growling

♥ Cute to Evil Grin

♥ Cute to Tongue

♥ Cute to Doofus

♥ Mini

NAME: Scarin' Erin

AKA: a butterfly

BIRTHDAY: December 22

LIKES: Skydiving. Metamorphosis. The Eiffel Tower.

I WOULD ALWAYS . . . go skydiving with Rude Alf, and not just because he likes it too. That nose is very helpful!

DISLIKES: Cats (they think we taste like chicken). Nets. Propellers.

I WOULD NEVER . . . tell a friend they tasted like chicken.

FAVORITE FOOD: Butterfingers

FAVORITE ACTIVITY: Bustin' out of the chrysalis.

WHAT EVERYBODY KNOWS: I got a tattoo of a lady's ankle on my wing.

WHAT NOBODY KNOWS: I used to look like a creepy worm.

BEST ADVICE: Don't fly above cats.

MOTTO/QUOTE: "Be fly like me!"

WHICH SCARIN' ERIN FEISTY PETS DO YOU HAVE?

🐾 Cute to Growling

🐾 Cute to Evil Grin

🐾 Cute to Tongue

🐾 Cute to Doofus

🐾 Mini

NAME: Sir Growls-a-Lot

AKA: a grizzly bear

BIRTHDAY: August 9

LIKES: Trash cans. Raw meat. Hibernating.

I WOULD ALWAYS . . . save the day, even at night! *Super Doofus!*

DISLIKES: Waking up. Loud noises. Jail food.

I WOULD NEVER . . . actually save the day.

FAVORITE FOOD: Rocky road ice cream.

FAVORITE ACTIVITY: Playing with matches.

WHAT EVERYBODY KNOWS: I change into a superhero in the toilet!

WHAT NOBODY KNOWS: Talking bears freak me out.

BEST ADVICE: Make sure no one is in the toilet before flushing it . . .

MOTTO/QUOTE: "This is a job for Super Doofus!"

WHICH SIR GROWLS-A-LOT FEISTY PETS DO YOU HAVE?

🐾 Cute to Growling

🐾 Cute to Evil Grin

🐾 Cute to Tongue

🐾 Cute to Doofus

🐾 Mini

81

NAME: Sly Sissypants

AKA: a red fox

BIRTHDAY: June 9

LIKES: Laser tag. Raiding trash cans. Playing with matches.

I WOULD ALWAYS . . . take advantage of a situation.

DISLIKES: Barbed-wire fences. Middle school. Pumpkin lattes.

I WOULD NEVER . . . take advantage of a friend . . . good thing I only have enemies.

FAVORITE FOOD: Any fast food—like rabbits.

FAVORITE ACTIVITY: Getting away unseen.

WHAT EVERYBODY KNOWS: If you want to get away with something, give me a call.

WHAT NOBODY KNOWS: I don't understand my last name. I'm not a sissy and I don't wear pants.

BEST ADVICE: Plan in the sunlight. Execute in the dark.

MOTTO/QUOTE: "Fox rocks!"

AKA: a Pegasus

BIRTHDAY: 750 BC

LIKES: Toga parties. Greek food. Butterflies. (They taste like chicken.)

I WOULD ALWAYS . . . give to horse charities. I feel so sorry for those poor little land-based mammals.

DISLIKES: Missiles. Heights. Imaginary creatures.

I WOULD NEVER . . . trust the government.

FAVORITE FOOD: Not rainbows—I tend to barf them up.

FAVORITE ACTIVITY: Battling rogue unicorns.

WHAT EVERYBODY ~~KNOWS~~ Needs to Know Horses are just less-cool Pegasi (that's Pegasus plural, duh!).

WHAT NOBODY KNOWS: I am against pixie dust.

BEST ADVICE: Always fly under the radar.

MOTTO/QUOTE: "Unicorns are overrated."

WHICH SPARKLES
RAINBOWBARF FEISTY PETS
DO YOU HAVE?

🐾 Cute to Growling

🐾 Cute to Evil Grin

🐾 Cute to Tongue

🐾 Cute to Doofus

🐾 Mini

NAME: Suzie Swearjar

AKA: a pig

BIRTHDAY: March 1

LIKES: Mud baths. Bacon. Aromatherapy.

MIS-UNDER-STOOD

I WOULD ALWAYS . . . pay up when I owe the swear jar . . . which I pretty much always do.

DISLIKES: Old MacDonald. Jogging. Bubble baths.

I WOULD NEVER . . . diet.

FAVORITE FOOD: Donuts—eaten with a knife and fork as a sign of respect.

FAVORITE ACTIVITY: You guess. Here are a couple hints: It involves MUD. It involves LAYING DOWN. Go!

WHAT EVERYBODY KNOWS: Pigs are geniuses.

WHAT NOBODY KNOWS: I AM actually afraid of the big bad wolf.

BEST ADVICE: Never wrestle with a pig. You both get filthy and the pig likes it.

MOTTO/QUOTE: "Don't be a *boar*!"

WHICH SUZIE SWEARJAR FEISTY PETS DO YOU HAVE?

- Cute to Growling
- Cute to Evil Grin
- Cute to Tongue
- Cute to Doofus
- Mini

NAME: Taylor Truelove

AKA: a valentine bear

BIRTHDAY: The day I discovered Taylor Swift.

LIKES: Freedom. Jacuzzis. Breakup songs.

I WILL ALWAYS . . . remember Taylor Swift . . .

DISLIKES: Long walks on the beach. Holding hands. Chocolates.

I WILL NEVER . . . forgive Katy Perry.

FAVORITE FOOD: I'll have what Taylor Swift is having.

FAVORITE ACTIVITY: Listening to Taylor Swift.

WHAT EVERYBODY KNOWS: Taylor Swift is a goddess.

WHAT NOBODY KNOWS: I love Taylor Swift. (Okay, so maybe you already know that, but I'm not going to miss an opportunity to say it again!)

BEST ADVICE: Be like Taylor Swift.

MOTTO/QUOTE: "I love you . . . to DEATH!"

R.I.P.
The Fourth
to Fall.

DO YOU HAVE A
TAYLOR TRUELOVE
FEISTY PET?

Cute to Growling

AKA: a harp seal

BIRTHDAY: March 22

LIKES: Vegetarians. Icebergs. Base jumping.

I WOULD ALWAYS . . . travel by iceberg.

DISLIKES: Polar bears. Icebreaker ships. CrossFit.

I WOULD NEVER . . . waddle when there's the option to slide.

FAVORITE FOOD: Seafood. I see food and I eat it.

FAVORITE ACTIVITY: Luge.

WHAT EVERYBODY KNOWS: Seals rule!

WHAT NOBODY KNOWS: I think ears look funny.

BEST ADVICE: Travel by pack ice . . . it's the only way to go!

MOTTO/QUOTE: "Don't make me your seal of approval!"

WHICH TONY TUBBALARD FEISTY PETS DO YOU HAVE?

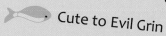 Cute to Growling

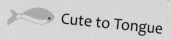 Cute to Evil Grin

 Cute to Tongue

Cute to Doofus

Mini

GO SEALS

NAME: Vicky Vicious

AKA: a bunny

BIRTHDAY: April 19

LIKES: Destroying gardens. Rap music. Chewing electrical cords.

I WOULD ALWAYS . . . steal your Easter basket.

DISLIKES: Cartoon characters. Easter. Your toes.

I WOULD NEVER . . . play with fire . . . unless it was nearby.

FAVORITE FOOD: The chihuahua's dinner.

FAVORITE ACTIVITY: Mosh pit dancing.

WHAT EVERYBODY KNOWS: I like to ROCK!

WHAT NOBODY KNOWS: My rapper name is Lil Vic.

BEST ADVICE: If you find yourself being filmed by the nature channel, and everybody is staring at you, and you aren't doing anything interesting—RUUUUUUN!!!!!

RIP Uncle Frank. PS I didn't see the wolf either.

MOTTO/QUOTE: "Let the bunnies hit the floor!"

92

WHICH VICKY VICIOUS FEISTY PETS DO YOU HAVE?

🐾 Cute to Growling

🐾 Cute to Evil Grin

🐾 Cute to Tongue

🐾 Cute to Doofus

🐾 Mini

AUTOGRAPHS

Vicky Vicious

Glenda Glitterpoop

Tony Tubbalard

Scarin' Erin

Taylor Truelove

FERDINAND FLAMEFART

Dastardly Daniel

Lightning Bolt Lenny

ICE Cold IZZY

Lethal Lena

Buford Buttsniffer

Lady Monstertruck

katy cobweb

Sparkles Rainbowbarf

Mary Monstertruck

HENRY WHodUNNit

JunkYard Jeff

Dolly Llama

Freddy Wreckingball

Ebeneezer ClawA

KARL THE SNARL

JACKED-Up JACKIE

Sammy Suckerpunch

Rascal Rampage

GRANDMASTER FUNK

Cuddles von Rumblestrut

RUDE ALF

Ali Cornball

MARKY MISCHIEF

Black Belt Bobby

Sir Growls-a-Lot

Louie Ladykiller

LUNATIC LEXI

Ginormous Gracie

Ali Cornball

Brainless Brian

Princess Pottymouth

Extinct Eddie

Sly Sissypants

Evil Eden

Billy Blubberbutt

Liza LOCA

Suzie Swearjar